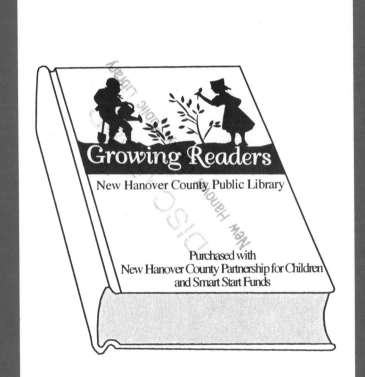

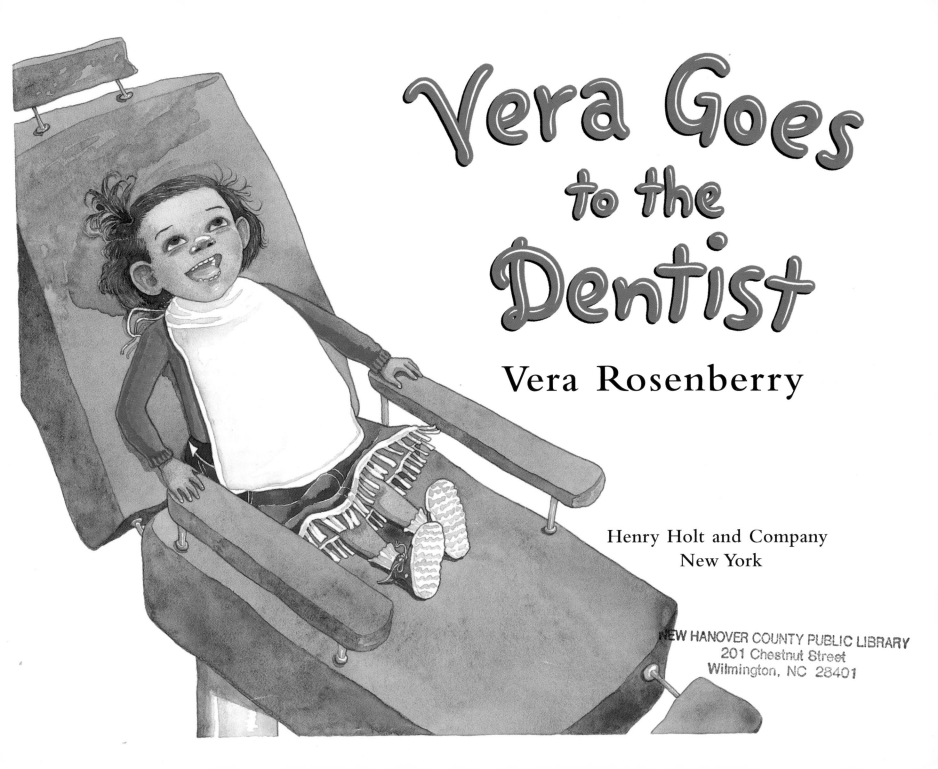

Vera Goes to the Dentist

Vera Rosenberry

Henry Holt and Company
New York

Henry Holt and Company, LLC
Publishers since 1866
115 West 18th Street
New York, New York 10011

Henry Holt is a registered trademark
of Henry Holt and Company, LLC
Copyright © 2002 by Vera Rosenberry
All rights reserved.
Distributed in Canada by
H. B. Fenn and Company Ltd.

Library of Congress Cataloging-in-Publication Data
Rosenberry, Vera.
Vera goes to the dentist / Vera Rosenberry.
Summary: On Vera's first visit to the dentist, she has an
unexpected reaction when he tries to polish her teeth.
[1. Dentists—Fiction.] I. Title.
PZ7.R719155 Vc 2002 [E]—dc21 2001000077

ISBN 0-8050-6668-3
First Edition—2002
Printed in the United States of America on acid-free paper. ∞

1 3 5 7 9 10 8 6 4 2

The artist used gouache on Lanaquarelle paper
to create the illustrations for this book.

June smiled into a mirror. She held a new purple toothbrush in her hand. "Look at my beautiful white teeth," she said to Vera. Then June sat and read her book. Vera waited. She wished her turn would come soon.

After a long time Elaine came out clutching a yellow toothbrush.

"Vera?" called the woman. "It's your turn." Vera followed her through the wooden door, just like her sisters had done.

She led Vera to a big chair. Vera sat down, and then the woman pressed a button. The big chair rose up. Vera felt very tall. The woman tied a white bib around her neck. "Dr. Knoll will be right with you," she said.

Vera looked around. There was an enormous window in front of her. Lots of bottles and jars were on a counter near a sink. There were some machines and it smelled funny, like minty medicine. Finally Dr. Knoll came into the room.

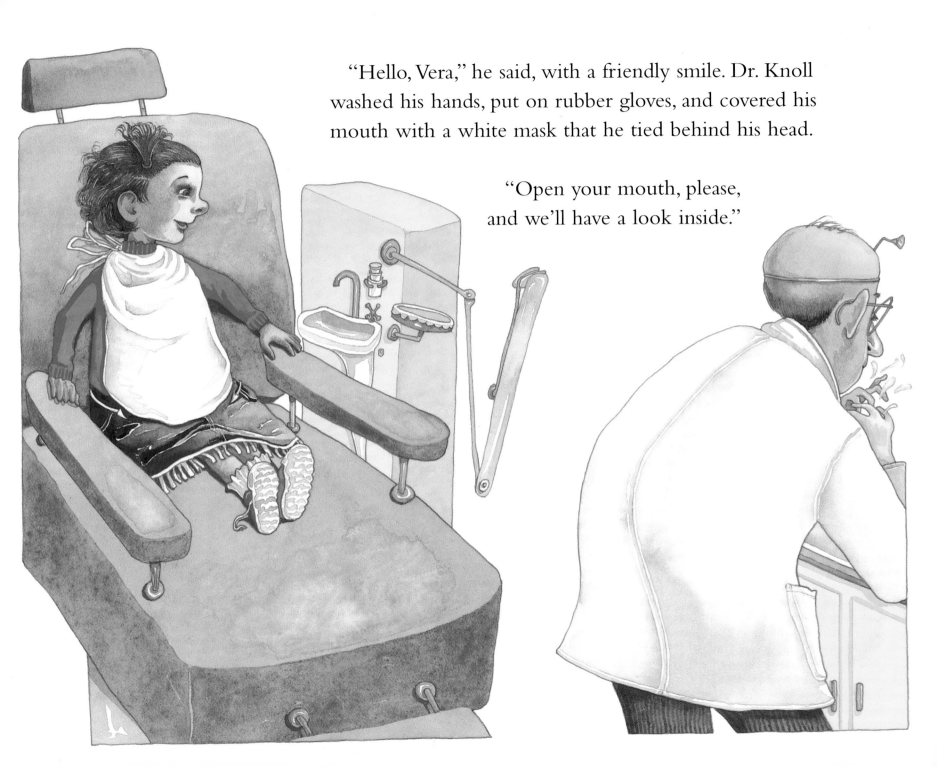

"Hello, Vera," he said, with a friendly smile. Dr. Knoll washed his hands, put on rubber gloves, and covered his mouth with a white mask that he tied behind his head.

"Open your mouth, please, and we'll have a look inside."

Vera opened her mouth. Dr. Knoll came very close to her. His glasses gleamed. He shined a light into her mouth with one hand as he held a tiny mirror in the other. Then he poked around her teeth with a pointy tool, but it didn't hurt.

"Everything looks just fine, Vera," said Dr. Knoll. "Let's clean your teeth, and you'll be all done for today."

He walked her out to the waiting room.
"Will you come and see me again?"

"Yes," said Vera. "Thank you for cleaning
my teeth. Good-bye." They shook hands.

Vera looked at her bright white smile in the mirrors as she and her family walked through the waiting room. She held her new green toothbrush up to admire it.

Going to the dentist was not the same as flying a kite with her father. Vera hoped she could do that on Sunday. But today it felt nice to have sparkling clean teeth.